THE
ABC
BUNNY

THE ABC BUNNY

By **WANDA GAG**

HAND LETTERED BY HOWARD GAG

PUBLISHED IN NEW YORK BY
COWARD-McCANN, INC.

LCC: 33-27359   ISBN: 0-698-20000-4 (hardcover trade edition)
ISBN: 0-698-20465-4 (pbk)
First paperback edition published October 1978
Printed in the U.S.A.
Twenty-seventh Impression (hardcover)
Fourth Impression (paperback)

SONG

N for Napping in a nook, O for Owl with bookish look. P for prickly Porc-u-pine
T for Tripping back to Town

Tra la la la la la la, Pins and needles on his spine, Tra la la la la la la
Tra la la la la la la, **U** for Up and Up-side-down, Tra la la la la la la

Q for Quail, **R** for Rail, **S** for Squirrel Swishy-tail, welcome you!" Tra la la la
V for View, Val-ley too, **W** —— "We

la la la, Squirrel Swishy-tail tra la.   **X** for eXit— off, away!
la la la, Welcome you, tra la tra la.

That's enough for us to-day, **Y** for You, take one last look, **Z** for Zero— close the book!

A

for Apple, big and red

B

for Bunny snug a-bed

C for Crash!

D for Dash!

E

for Elsewhere in a flash

F

for Frog – he's fat and funny

"Looks like rain," says he to Bunny

G for Gale!

H for Hail!

Hippy-hop goes Bunny's tail

I

for Insects here and there

J

for Jay with jaunty air

K

for Kitten , catnip-crazy

L

for Lizard – look how lazy

M

for Mealtime – munch , munch , munch

M-m-m! these greens are good for lunch

N

for Napping in a Nook

O

for Owl with bookish look

P

for prickly Porcupine

Pins and needles on his spine

Q for Quail

R for Rail

S

for Squirrel Swishy-tail

T

for Tripping back to Town

U

for Up and Up-side-down

V for View

Valley too

W

—"We welcome you!"

 for eXit — off, away!

That's enough for us today

Y

for You , take one last look

Z

for Zero — close the book!

ABC

MUSIC BY FLAVIA GÁG

A for Ap-ple big and red, Tra la la la la la la, B for Bun-ny
F for Frog—he's fat and funny, Tra la la la la la la, "Looks like rain," says

snug a-bed, Tra la la la la la la, C for Crash! D for Dash! E for Elsewhere
he to Bun-ny, Tra la la la la la la, G for Gale! H for Hail! Hip-py hop goes

rit.

in a flash Tra la la la la la la la, Elsewhere in a flash, tra la. I for Insects
Bunny's tail Tra la la la la la la la, Hip-py hip-py hop, tra la.

here and there J for Jay with jaunty air K for Kitten catnip-crazy L for Lizard—

Look how lazy! M for Meal time— munch, munch, munch! M-m-m! these greens are good for lunch

WANDA GÁG (1893-1946) was born in New Ulm, Minnesota. As a child she was surrounded by an almost European atmosphere of old world customs and legends, of Bavarian and Bohemian folk songs.

The daughter of a Bohemian artist and the eldest of the seven Gág children, Wanda was part of a family that sparkled with creativity. Drawing and story-telling were as much a part of her life as eating and sleeping, and she was surprised to grow up and find that there were some people who did not draw at all.

Wanda Gág created THE ABC BUNNY in 1933 for Gary, her small nephew. And, as part of a talented family's work, the "ABC Song" which appears with the text was composed by Flavia Gág, Wanda's sister. The text was hand-lettered by Howard Gág, her brother.

In recognition of Wanda Gág's artistry, she was posthumously awarded the 1958 Lewis Carroll Shelf Award for her 1928 picture book, MILLIONS OF CATS, and the 1977 Kerlan Award for the body of her work, which includes THE FUNNY THING, GONE IS GONE, NOTHING AT ALL, SNIPPY AND SNAPPY, SNOW WHITE AND THE SEVEN DWARFS, TALES FROM GRIMM, and MORE TALES FROM GRIMM.